BONES!

PAUL SHIPTON

Illustrated by Andy Hammond

£ 2.50

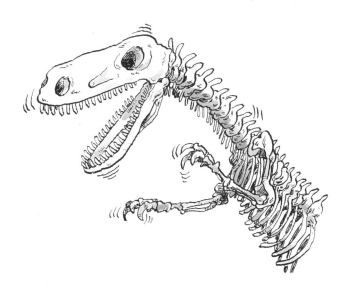

OXFORD
UNIVERSITY PRESS

OXFORD

UNIVERSITY PRESS

Great Clarendon Street, Oxford OX2 6DP

Oxford University Press is a department of the University of Oxford.
It furthers the University's objective of excellence in research, scholarship,
and education by publishing worldwide in

Oxford   New York

Auckland   Cape Town   Dar es Salaam   Hong Kong   Karachi
Kuala Lumpur   Madrid   Melbourne   Mexico City   Nairobi
New Delhi   Shanghai   Taipei   Toronto

With offices in

Argentina   Austria   Brazil   Chile   Czech Republic   France   Greece
Guatemala   Hungary   Italy   Japan   Poland   Portugal   Singapore
South Korea   Switzerland   Thailand   Turkey   Ukraine   Vietnam

Oxford is a registered trade mark of Oxford University Press
in the UK and in certain other countries

British Library Cataloguing in Publication Data
Data available

ISBN-13: 978-0-19-918388-3
ISBN-10: 0-19-918388-0

3 5 7 9 10 8 6 4 2

Available in packs
Stage 13 More Stories A Pack of 6:
ISBN-13: 978-0-19-918386-9; ISBN-10: 0-19-918386-4
Stage 13 More Stories A Class Pack:
ISBN-13: 978-0-19-918393-7; ISBN-10: 0-19-918393-7
Guided Reading Cards also available:
ISBN-13: 978-0-19-918395-1; ISBN-10: 0-19-918395-3

Cover artwork by Andy Hammond

Printed in China by Imago

Something is wrong

'Chris? Are you in here?'

David's voice echoed around the room. There was no reply. He went further inside. The room looked empty. The rest of the class had moved on to other parts of the museum – all except David and Chris.

David stood next to a glass case full of fossils. This was where they had agreed to meet… so where was Chris?

He glanced at his watch and
wondered what to do. He was about to
go on by himself, when a sudden feeling
crept over him that something was
wrong here. An icy chill tickled the back
of his neck. He couldn't tell what, but
something was wrong! David began to
stride towards the exit when –

A blur of movement caught his eye.

David let out a yell of fear and jumped back. (It would have been an Olympic-record long jump if it had been forwards instead of backwards.)

It was Chris – he had been hiding behind a pillar. His grin covered most of his face.

David's heart was thumping.

He couldn't understand why jumping out and scaring someone was supposed to be funny.

Chris's grin stretched wider. 'You should have seen the look on your face.'

He leaned forward as if he were giving away an important secret. 'It's all in the timing, you know,' he said proudly.

David sighed.
Why did he have to get the class joker as a partner for the museum trip?

That's why David and Chris were so far behind the others. The class had to go round the museum in pairs with a worksheet. But David and Chris weren't a very good team. David spent too long looking at everything. By the time he'd finished, he had forgotten all about the question on the worksheet.

Chris, on the other hand… He was too busy making jokes all the time.

In the Egyptian Room he made jokes about wanting his *mummy*. In the Medieval Room he made jokes about knights going to *knight school*.

It was enough to drive David crazy.

Chris held up his crumpled worksheet now. David saw a chocolate thumb-print and a messy doodle on it. But no answers.

David *almost* said: 'Can't you do ANYTHING right, except make stupid jokes?' But he didn't.

He and Chris had been good friends when they were little. Now they didn't see each other much any more, but David still didn't want to hurt his friend's feelings.

They walked over to a large glass case. Chris held his pencil at the ready.

But David didn't move. His mind was filled with wonder.

Chris shrugged. He looked as if it was just a crummy old lump of rock to him.

But David didn't even hear this bad joke. He gasped in amazement.

It was the asteroid. A tiny red crack had appeared in it. The boys watched in ✳ <u>awe</u> as the crack grew longer. Smaller cracks began to break off from it. It looked like the frost pattern on a window in winter, except these cracks glowed with a red light.

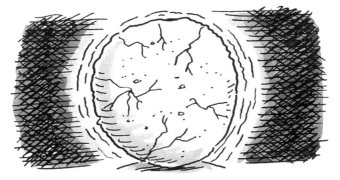

Almost as if there was something inside...

Something trying to get out.

Chris glanced nervously at David.

What's going...

Before he could finish the question, the air was filled with a chorus of screams. They were coming from the main hall of the museum.

HELP!! HELP!! CLUNK AAAGH! HELP!! RUN FOR IT! LOOK OUT! CRASH CLUNK CLUNK!

Underneath the cries, there was another sound – the sound of something hard, like metal, hitting the museum's marble floor.

The bones come alive

The two boys rushed to look down into the main hall below. David couldn't believe what he saw.

Their teacher and all the kids in their class were charging across the floor in terror. Behind them came a gigantic dinosaur!

Well, not quite a dinosaur. It was the *skeleton* of a dinosaur – a triceratops.

It had been standing near the
entrance to the main hall, as if it were
guarding the museum. But now it was
moving slowly forward.

The bones had come to life!

The noise David and Chris could hear
was the sound of bone tapping on
marble. The massive beast's joints
creaked as it plodded on. It kept its head
down and pointed its three horns at the
panicking children.

David was mumbling in disbelief.
Chris clutched his arm.
The two boys whirled around.

There was another dinosaur skeleton on the move – perhaps the most fearsome dinosaur of all, a tyrannosaurus rex. And it was coming their way!

Though it had no eyes, it seemed to see them. It snapped its massive jaws together and speeded up. Its bony tail waved from side to side.

David couldn't move. He was
frozen in fear like a rabbit in the path
of on-coming headlights.

But Chris shoved him and he came to his senses. The terrified boys ran for their lives.

They fled towards one of the smaller rooms that were all around the upper main hall. In his panic, David slipped on the polished floor and stumbled.

He looked back and saw the T. rex loom closer. It was almost upon him. Its huge head swooped low and David saw its jagged teeth. There were LOTS of them.

Even in his fear, an odd thought strayed into David's mind. He would only be a light snack for the beast – about as filling as a bag of crisps, maybe.

He scrambled to his knees and charged away like a sprinter. He felt a rush of cold air behind him – something very big was moving very fast.

He could see Chris up ahead, looking back in wide-eyed terror. David made it through the archway into a side room.

An instant later, there was a huge

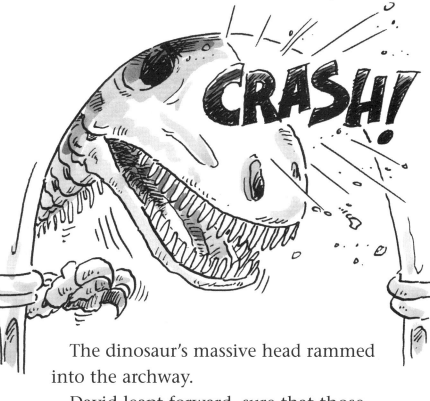

The dinosaur's massive head rammed into the archway.

David leapt forward, sure that those enormous jaws were about to close around him.

21

But they didn't.

David rolled onto his side and saw why. The huge beast was too big to get through the archway into the side room. It could poke its head in a little way, but that was as far as it could get.

David scrambled to his feet. His legs were trembling. He and Chris looked in frightened awe at the dinosaur. It seemed to be looking back at them from the blackness of its empty eye sockets.

Chris smiled weakly and shook his fist at the giant creature of bone.

Let that be a lesson to you!

Nobody laughed.

The two boys edged
further back into the safety of
the smaller room. They began to
catch their breath. David felt dizzy with
fear. His brain almost refused to accept
what was going on. It just wasn't
possible. Chris looked shaken.

We're safe in here, aren't we? Just as long as we don't go near the main hall...

David began to nod slowly... but then
he spotted it.

One of the platforms in the room was empty except for a few scattered metal rods. The sign at the base of the platform said VELOCIRAPTOR.

Fear squeezed David's heart again.

'Stop!' he whispered to Chris. He looked slowly around the room. Nothing moved. There was no sound apart from the tapping of the tyrannosaurus' claws outside. Or was there? Could he hear a low rustle from somewhere inside the room?

Suddenly he saw a flash of white. A clattering noise. There WAS something in here, and David knew what. 'Run!' he yelled.

Terrified, they ran headlong through the next two rooms and into the one beyond that.

This was the Medieval Room. A model of a knight on a horse sat in the middle of the room, and rows of knights in armour stood along either side.

'Where now?' panted Chris.

It was a good question. The only other way out of this room led back to the upper main hall… and the waiting tyrannosaurus. They had gone in a semi-circle. They couldn't go forward. But what lay behind them?

David scurried across to one of the suits of armour. He was frantically trying to pull an axe from a knight's grip. Chris joined him.

David, what's a velociraptor?

David gave a grim look and kept on tugging at the axe.

'Raptors? They're bad news.

He knew that velociraptors were dinosaurs that used their strong front arms to grasp victims. Then they attacked them with the claws on each back foot. David explained that they walked on two legs like the tyrannosaurus, but they were only the size of a tall human.

Chris blinked, taking it all in.

But... if they're not so big, maybe we can fight them?

David shook his head.

'Raptors were savage killers — we wouldn't stand a chance. The fact that they're not very big just means one thing...

He paused and glanced at the axe in his hand. It would be no more use as a weapon than a banana would be.

...they can follow us anywhere.

So what are we going to do?

But at that moment they heard a sound behind them. The walking skeleton of a velociraptor was standing in the doorway.

It scanned the room with the quick head movements of a hawk – the hunter looking for its prey. Its razor-like teeth seemed fixed in a grin.

All of David's instincts told him to run. But he forced himself not to. After all, where could they run to?

He clamped a hand onto Chris's arm. Both boys stood still. They were hidden from the 'raptor by the knights in armour.

The 'raptor was inside the room now. It was making its way right down the middle. The only sound was the tap of its claws and the scrape of its dragging tail.

The beast was halfway through the room. It still hadn't seen the boys.

Maybe they could escape? thought David. And that's when he felt it – a faint tickle at the back of his nose. It got stronger. A sneeze was on its way.

He bit down on his lip and held his breath. He told himself, *Don't sneeze, please don't sneeze.*

The 'raptor went on its slow prowl through the room. It had gone past the boys' hiding place now. In another couple of minutes it would be gone.

But the sneeze could wait no longer.

David tried to swallow it back – his head nodded slightly with the force of it, but he made no noise. He opened his mouth to take in air and a second sneeze caught him by surprise. This one sounded like a small explosion in the silence of the museum room.

The 'raptor whirled around. Its eyeless stare fell on the boys' hiding place. The chase was back on!

Chris and David pelted out knocking one of the suits of armour over. It tumbled forward with a clatter. The boys didn't look back at the dinosaur. They knew it would be racing down the room towards them.

Then Chris stopped.

Chris didn't answer. He turned towards the charging dinosaur.

David watched in terror and
amazement. A lethal dinosaur was
hurtling towards Chris, but he didn't
move! Did he want to become a
dinosaur's dinner?

The 'raptor picked up speed and
jumped into the air. This was it – in for
the kill!

At the *very* last moment Chris threw
himself flat.

The 'raptor sailed over his head – straight on to the <u>lance </u>of the dummy knight on horseback. There was an enormous crash of bone hitting metal.

A shower of splintering bone fell on Chris's back. He huddled into a ball. He was waiting for the final blow to come.

But it didn't.

The creature was gone. It had smashed apart. It was now just a pile of bones scattered across the floor.

Slowly Chris uncurled. Then he looked at David and grinned.

For once, David didn't mind one of Chris's rotten jokes.

Chris smiled and tapped the side of his nose.

'But what's behind all of this?' said David. He felt as if his brain was exploding. Then, in a flash, he knew where they could find the answers.

The asteroid! This all started with that asteroid. We need to get back to that room.

Chris didn't look too happy at the idea.

But can't we just hide out now? Wait for the police or something?

Before David could answer, there was a quick movement on the floor. One of the broken 'raptor claws twitched and grabbed hold of Chris's ankle.

David bent down and tried to pull the claw off. But its grip was too strong. He began to hit it with the axe which was still in his hand.

Then he saw that the other bits of bone were stirring. They were slowly moving as if… as if they were going to put themselves back together!

This thought gave him added strength. He gave the claw a final mighty bash with the axe.

It let go for an instant – long enough for Chris to pull his leg away.

The two boys ran. 'OK,' panted Chris. 'Let's go back there.'

There was just one problem. To get to the asteroid they would have to run through the upper hall. Just the thought of what waited there made David's legs turn to jelly.

They peered out.

The tyrannosaurus was down at the far end. It was patrolling the hall like an enthusiastic security guard.

They dashed out. David heard that horrible tap of bone on marble behind them, but he did not even look back. He kept his head and charged onwards.

The two boys burst into the room with the asteroid. They had outrun the huge dinosaur. But their problems weren't over yet. In fact, they had only just begun…

Who are you?

The glass case that had held the asteroid
was broken open. A ball of light hovered
in the air, about three metres from the
ground.

When the two boys ran into the
room, the ball of light glowed a deeper
red. It floated down to their eye-level.
Somehow, David knew that it was
aware of them.

Suddenly a voice echoed inside their minds. It sounded like hundreds of voices all speaking at once – it reminded David of the hum of a hive of bees. He knew the voice was coming from the light, which was glowing brighter now.

STOP THERE, HUMANS.

It was an effort to speak, but David managed to get a question out.

Wh-who are you?

This didn't sound good. David
glanced at Chris. He looked worried too.

Suddenly the ball of light let out a high-pitched buzz. The noise seemed to burn right through David's brain. He could hardly think.

45

At last the buzzing ended. After a long pause, the voice spoke again:

WE HAVE MADE OUR JUDGEMENT. WE HAVE FOUND YOU HUMANS TO BE A POOR, SAD LITTLE SPECIES. THE SENTENCE IS.... TOTAL DESTRUCTION. THIS PLANET WILL BE DESTROYED IN ONE MINUTE.

David jumped forward. 'Wait!' he shouted. 'You can't just destroy us. Look at all the good things we've done.'

There was another pause before the voice boomed inside his head again.

WHAT THINGS?

The alien was not impressed.

David looked down. He was still gripping the axe.

The alien went on.

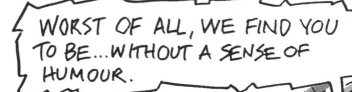

WORST OF ALL, WE FIND YOU
TO BE...WITHOUT A SENSE OF
HUMOUR.

Chris had stayed silent as if he was
simply too amazed to say anything.
But now he jumped to attention when
the alien said 'sense of humour'.

He stepped forward with
determination.

He sounded as if the suggestion had deeply offended him.

He drew a deep breath and... nothing. The future of the planet depended on one of his jokes. But Chris, the boy who made jokes all the time, could not come up with a single joke.

Um... wait a minute.

But they didn't have a minute! Chris looked blank. And the only thing David could think of was something about a chicken and a road.

David glanced nervously at his watch – just ten seconds until the minute was up. This was it – the end of the world!

Chris cried out.

Wait!
I've got one!

He rushed forward eagerly.

His foot skidded on the polished
marble floor.

He flipped up into the air and landed
with a yell of surprise on his backside.

All was quiet for several seconds.

Then suddenly the ball of light turned a deeper shade of red. David's mind was filled with a sound like a flock of seagulls shrieking. It didn't sound much like laughter, and yet somehow he knew that was what it was. Then the voice spoke once again in his brain.

NOW **THAT** WAS FUNNY! ALMOST AS FUNNY AS BRINGING THE BONES TO LIFE.

David couldn't believe his ears. Did this alien think that bringing the bones to life was a joke?

CLEARLY YOU **DO** HAVE A SENSE OF HUMOUR. OUR DECISION IS REVERSED. FAREWELL!

There was a loud crackle and a flash of blue lightning.

When the stars were no longer dancing before his eyes and David could see again, the ball of light was gone.

David looked at Chris in admiration.

Chris got to his feet.

He was red-faced and angry. It seemed that his pride was hurt more than his backside.

David and Chris walked back towards the main hall. David could hear the voices of their classmates in the distance, but he knew that the dinosaurs would once again be no more than unmoving bones.

The aliens had gone to play their jokes on the next planet they visited... and to make judgement there.

David suddenly had a terrible thought.

Chris's grin returned at last.

About the author

When I was growing up in Manchester, I always wanted to be an astronaut, a footballer, or (if those didn't work out for any reason) perhaps a rock star. So it came as something of a shock when I  became first a teacher and then an editor of educational books.

I have lived in Cambridge, Aylesbury, Oxford and Istanbul. I'm still on the run and now live in Chicago with my wife and family.

I can remember long afternoons spent wandering the rooms of the museum near my house. I'm sure this story – or something like it – first came to me on one of those afternoons.